Y0-AAR-123

Disney · PIXAR

INSIDE OUT

FEAR

by **Brittany Candau**
illustrated by **Jerrod Maruyama**

DISNEP PRESS
Los Angeles · New York

H-hello!

I'm Fear.

I consider every day we don't die a success.

Especially since the world is full of terrifying things.

Gum
Flower
Vacuum
Swings
Mustard
Curtains
light
Window
Bunnies
Dust
Leaves
Salt
Ice
Ruby
Pebb
Hallo
Seash
Pasta
Floss
Kittens
Chalk

Look!
I have a list!

There's the stairs to the basement . . .

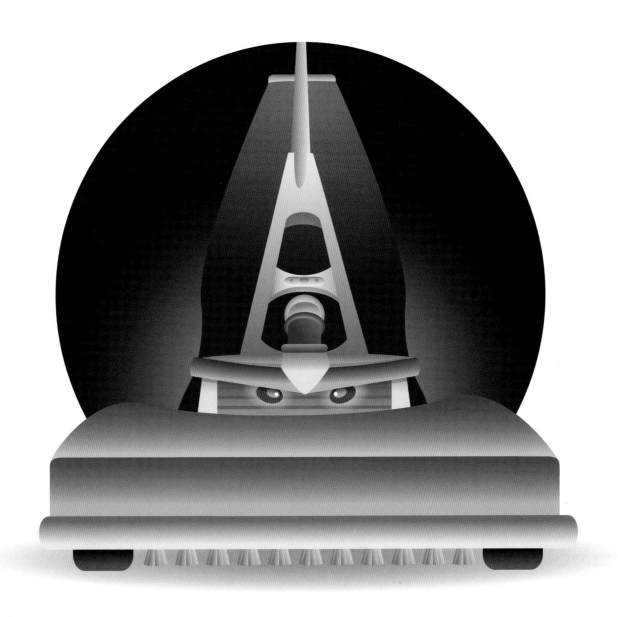

**and Grandma's
vacuum cleaner . . .**

and, dare I even say it...

CLOWNS!

It's my job to keep us safe from such perils.

Like making everyone aware that sliding down banisters is very dangerous business.

But no one listens to me. We could lose a tooth or something! Is it worth it, people?

It's a thankless job. Somebody's gotta do it.
But let me tell you what I do like....

I like
SAFETY!

I like being surrounded by soft things, like feathers and marshmallows. Oh, and **socks**!

And I

LOVE

to relax in the evenings, sip a cup of tea, and watch a peaceful nature show. . . .

AHHH

HHHH!

Awww!
What a cute little hippo!